AF448466

THIS BOOK BELONGS TO

ICON

Icon Publishing Limited
P. O. Box OD 972
Odorkor, Accra
Ghana
www.facebook.com/myicongh
www.twitter.com/myicongh
+233 (0)23 3505 055,

iconpublishingltd@gmail.com
iconpublishing@ymail.com
enquiries.icongh@gmail.com

Books published by Icon Publishing Limited are available at special discounts for bulk purchases in Ghana by corporations, institutions, and other organisations. For more information, please call the Special Markets Department on +233 (0)23 3505 055 or send an e-mail to iconpublishingltd@gmail.com.

Cover and Interior Design by iCON-gh +233 24 4890 432

ISBN: 978-9988-8566-6-3

JEALOUSY BETWEEN THE TWIN SISTERS

A GHANAIAN FOLKTALE

Dan Odei

Kwame Insaidoo

This Ghanaian folktale shows the evils of sibling rivalry and the end result of jealousy.

Many years ago, there lived two beautiful twin sisters. The elder was called Apani, while the younger was called Akuma. They lived in a big house with their parents until they passed on to be with their maker.

After their parents' deaths, the sisters were left alone since they were without husbands and did not have any other family members, but they were happy and did many things together. They loved each other, treated each other with the utmost respect, and always ensured that no one came between them. Each looked for the other before she went to sleep to ensure that everything was okay with the other sister, and people in the town were always delighted to see them together.

One day the younger twin, Akuma, found her soul mate; so the two decided to seal their love in marriage, and they made all the necessary arrangements for the great day. During the wedding ceremony, Akuma's elder twin loaned her sister a splendid golden necklace bedecked with numerous diamonds, and she looked regal, just like the queen of the town. This made her elder sister jealous and filled her with envy. She began to wish that she had her own husband, and she muttered to herself, "I will even get a more handsome husband than my sister." And with that she concealed her venomous jealousy towards her own twin sister. With her heart still reeking and fuming with concealed jealousy of her twin sister, she attended the wedding and pretended that everything was alright and she was enjoying herself.

Apani accompanied and chaperoned her twin sister with fanfare during the entire wedding ceremony, and her younger sister, Akuma, unaware that her twin sister was fuming with jealousy, was grateful that her only sister was by her side during the most important day of her life.

The ceremony and the fanfare gradually wound down at the end of the day, but the bride was still euphoric about marrying her soul mate. She was intoxicated with joy and did not notice that her sister's golden necklace, which was encrusted with diamonds, had fallen into a small stream with swift currents.

When Akuma reached home, she felt sick to her stomach when she discovered that she could not find the necklace. The more she looked for it, the sicker she got, as the necklace was nowhere to be found. She wept bitterly, knowing that the necklace was too expensive to lose. She did not know what her older sister would say or do to her, but she summoned her courage and, her voice choked with tears, informed her sister that she had lost her necklace.

Apani pretended that she had not heard her sister's words correctly and asked her to repeat herself. As Akuma said again that she had lost the necklace, she interrupted her and asked, "You what? You mean to say you were so taken by that ugly husband of yours that you lost my heirloom, a necklace given to me by our dead mother? What is the matter with you? Were you so drunk that you could not safeguard my precious necklace?"

Apani did not eat for a whole day, claiming it was because she was saddened by the loss of the necklace, but many people around her knew that she was faking because of her intense jealousy of her sister who had lucked out and married the wealthiest man in the community. Apani, in her anger and jealousy,

Akuma searching for the lost necklace

told her sister that she would have to make a compensation for losing her precious necklace. Apani demanded three precious items from Akuma. She wanted her sister to give her the following: a silver canoe, a golden stick, and the tail of the queen of elephants, which was much sought after and signified wealth and membership in the upper echelon of their society.

When the younger sister heard the outrageous demands from her twin sister she knew in her heart that her sister was fuming with jealousy because of her successful marriage. She wept, not so much for the three items she had to compensate her with, but because she hated to destroy the loving relationship she had painstakingly built with her sister since infancy.

Despite all these melancholy thoughts running through her head, Akuma set out one hot afternoon to look for the precious compensation her sister demanded from her. She walked for many days through the bushes, crossed many rivers, and went to villages inhabited by enemies of her people, who were hostile to her. Before they could pounce on her however, she sang a pitiful song from her heart to the villagers:

When the hostile villagers heard her song, they were touched by the story she related to them; their hostility slowly melted away, and they became sympathetic to her cause. The chief and the people warned her not to come to the village again, but gave her the silver canoe and bade her farewell.

She sincerely thanked the chief and his people and then left the village early in the morning, continuing on foot through the bushes for many days. She was nearing exhaustion and dusk was approaching when she arrived at a small town inhabited only by men.

The men looked surprised to see a woman come to their town and asked what had brought her to their town, where no woman was supposed to come. As usual she sang her melancholy dirge about how she had lost her twin sister's golden necklace and her sister, in her cruelty, demanded a silver boat, a golden stick, and the tail of the queen of elephants.

The king of the town was touched by the miserable plight of Akuma, so he took her to her palace and gave her a golden stick, a diamond necklace, several gold nuggets, and bracelets made of gold and diamonds. Then he told her never to come to the town again because the gods did not want to see her kind in that town.

The next morning Akuma left the town and continued her search for the last item on her sister's list of demands; the tail of the elephant queen. She was instructed to travel toward the southern part of the city, where trees surrounded many lakes. She travelled for many days, crossing small lakes and rivers as she moved relentlessly toward the southern tier of the lakes and rivers. Finally, she reached a small hut inhabited by an old lady.

The old lady was astonished to see the face of a human in her village and told Akuma, "You see, my little daughter, you have committed an abomination by coming to my little hut. No human being has ever come to this place and returned alive. Why did you come to this forbidden place?" Akuma, fearful of the old lady, began to weep, and then she sang her melancholy song in answer to the old woman's question:

Our loving parents lived with us for many years
We were the only children they had
And unfortunately for us our parents passed on to the other side
And I decided to marry when my prince came knocking
The necklace I borrowed from my elder twin sister got lost
She was cruel to me and sent me away to compensate her with
A silver canoe, a golden stick, and the tail of the queen of elephants
And that is why I have come to your forbidden village
And if you want to kill me, this is the best time and place for I am tired

The old lady became sympathetic to Akuma and decided to help her get the tail of the queen of the elephants. She told Akuma that she was at the right place. "I live with the elephants, and they trust me enough that anything I tell them they listen to. But if they come here and see a human face, they will kill you, so I have to hide you in a hole under my kitchen till they go back to sleep."

The old lady fed Akuma and toward nightfall hid her in the small cave underneath her kitchen as she had promised. No sooner had she hidden Akuma than all the elephants descended on the old lady's hut. Upon sniffing around the hut, they began to complain loudly that they smelled a strange human scent in the hut. The old lady pretended that she was angry with the elephants for complaining about a human scent and bellowed, "Look, I am a human being with a human scent! If you are tired of me, kill me now and stop annoying me with your silly complaints."

The elephants apologized to the lady for their rude behaviour and asked her to forgive them. They stayed with her late into the night and then bade her farewell and proceeded to their sleeping place in the valley of the elephants.

Once all the elephants had left the hut, the old lady brought Akuma out and gave her a sharp knife and the following instructions:

"The elephants sleep in a long row, from one end of the valley to the other, and there are a total of one hundred elephants. Their queen is jet-black and is the last elephant in the row.

"You have to step as hard as you can on the elephants to get to the last one, the queen. If you do not step hard on them, you will wake them up, they will kill you, and nobody will ever hear of you again, including your beloved husband.

"You have to hide behind the trees near the southern lakes and listen for the sounds the elephants make. If you hear them making *'huruturu, huruturu, huruturu'* sounds, that means they are busy conversing. Do not go near them because they are not asleep and will eat you up.

"You have to continue to wait behind the large tree and listen until the elephants make *'wheetum, wheetum, wheetum,'* noises. That means they are fast asleep and snoring like frogs. Believe me, these large animals sleep deep, like they are dead, so walk as hard as you can on them. They will never feel or hear your footsteps. Good luck, my little one."

After receiving the old woman's instructions, Akuma took the knife and courageously went and hid behind the large trees near the southern lake as she had been told to. When she got there, she heard the elephants making, *"huruturu, huruturu"* sounds, and she kept so quiet that she could hear her own heart beat. Her heart was nearly in her mouth. After waiting for about another hour, she heard the elephants snoring noises, *"wheetum, wheetum,*

wheetum," and she knew the time for action was at hand.

She summoned all the courage she could, moved boldly, and stepped on the elephants as hard as she could, till she came to the queen. Without hesitation, she slashed off the queen's tail and ran as fast as she could back to the old lady's hut.

The old lady felt a kinship with Akuma and was glad to know that despite her twin sister's envy and cruelty to her she was ever determined to succeed. She gave Akuma some of her valuable golden nuggets, bracelets, gold rings, diamond necklaces, golden cups and plates, and other precious items as a marriage present and then bade her farewell. Akuma for her part was grateful to the old lady and thanked her for all she had done for her. She left the hut carrying all the gifts that had been showered on her. She ran through the bushes and followed the shortest possible route to her village, which the old lady had shown her.

Meanwhile, in the middle of the night, the elephants' fetish priest woke up with a shrill shout. In his dream he had seen a young girl cut off the tail of their queen. They all rushed to the queen's side and found her lying in a pool of blood. They took her to the old lady's hut, and the old lady applied some herbs. The cut healed instantly, but the elephants were upset with her because they knew she had betrayed them.

When Akuma reached her village she called all the villagers, including her twin sister, the chief, and elders to her house and began to sing:

You see, my fellow villagers, our parents had only the two of us, just us twins
Then they passed on to the other world that you don't come back from
I got lucky and married a wealthy and responsible man
My twin sister generously loaned me a beautiful necklace
That mysteriously got lost in a river with swift currents
She wept for days and asked me to compensate her
With a silver canoe, a golden stick, and the tail of the queen of the elephants
With the help of almighty God and all our ancestors who have gone before us
I went through bushes, lakes, rivers, mountaintops, and valleys of darkness
And eventually got all the things she cruelly demanded from me
Now in the presence of all of you as my witnesses
I present to her, the silver canoe, the golden stick

All the villagers applauded the younger sister, Akuma, as she gave all the items to her elder sister. After that Akuma and her husband went to their home to begin their much anticipated married life with all the precious gifts she had brought home—and they were nice enough to allow her elder sister, Apani, to move in with them.

One morning Akuma and her husband left very early in the morning to go to their farm to harvest their yams. They left Apani at home. Once they had left, Apani invited all her friends in the village to a party at her sister's house, because she wanted to impress her friends and show off all the golden necklaces, pots, sticks, cups, and other ornaments they had in the house. She served all her friends in the golden pots, pans, and cups belonging to her sister, and she also gave some of her sister's jewellery to her friends. Unfortunately, she also broke three of her sister's golden cups and did not know how she was going to explain it to Akuma when she came home.

When Akuma got home, she saw that three of her golden cups were broken, and she asked her elder twin sister what happened to them. The younger sister in her anger asked her elder sister to compensate her with a silver canoe, a golden stick, and the tail of the queen of elephants. The older sister could have compensated her with the same items she had already received from Akuma, but she wanted to prove to her that she was equally capable of getting those items on her own. So she promised her sister, "I'll be back in a week with your silly boat, your stick, and the tail of the crazy elephant queen. You know, if you could get all these things with your level of intelligence, how much more I, the elder sister, who has more wisdom than you?"

Apani, the elder twin sister, set foot into the bushes and walked for many days until she came to a village. The inhabitants asked what brought her to their village, and in her arrogance responded, "You bush people ask so many silly questions! Don't you know I am a queen from another village? You bush people, hurry up and bring me the silver canoe you gave my sister when she came here, because I am in a hurry and don't have time for your silly questions."

The villagers were amazed at her sauciness, arrogance, and rude attitude toward them, so they hurriedly gave her an inferior, cheaply made silver canoe and asked her to leave their village, adding, "You'll see what will happen to you in this world if you continue to be rude and act arrogantly toward people." Apani took her silver canoe and left, failing even to thank them because she could care less what the villagers thought about her. She said to herself, "The end justifies the means."

Apani set out for the next village, and when she got there, the villagers surrounded her and asked her what had brought her to their village. Apani began to scream and yell at them like they were her children, "What is your problem? Haven't you people ever seen a beautiful woman like me? Hurry up and bring me the golden stick you keep in your little ugly huts."

The villagers were astounded to hear how rudely she spoke to all of them, and they asked themselves if such saucy and rude humans actually lived on earth.

The villagers wanted her to leave their village and take all her troubles with her, so they gave her the cheapest of the golden sticks they had. She yanked it from their hands and took it away without bothering to thank them. The villagers were glad to get rid of her and her numerous problems, but before she left the village, she also took many of the gold necklaces, golden nuggets, and bracelets that were lying in the village's square. She carried them on top of her head, while dragging the silver canoe along behind her.

She eventually reached the village of the elephants and met the old lady, who was lost for words, amazed to see another young woman in her village. She summoned all the strength at her disposal to inquire why Apani had travelled so long to come to her village.

Apani rudely told her that she needed to get the tail of the queen of the elephants and that the old lady should hurry up and show her how to get the tail quickly so she could get back to her business in her own village. As she had told Akuma, the old lady instructed Apani to walk with all her strength on the elephants and look for the queen, who would be the last one sleeping at the end of the long row. She told Apani to be cautious because the last queen had lost her tail, and the elephants were jealously guarding their new queen and wouldn't want anything to happen to her. Furthermore, the old lady instructed her about the difference between the *"wheetum, wheetum, wheetum"* sounds of snoring and the *"huruturu, huruturu, huruturu"* sounds that meant they were not asleep but conversing among themselves. She gave Apani the sharp knife and warned her to wait until the elephants were asleep and snoring before going into their sleeping valley.

The elder sister waited for a long time till she heard the elephants snoring, and then she proceeded to the valley and saw a long row of sleeping elephants. But instead of following the old lady's instructions to walk heavily on the sleeping animals, she tip-toed over them till she reached the middle of the row. Then, all of a sudden, the fetish priest elephant woke up with a shrill noise, calling out that he saw a young woman trying to get to their new queen.

All the elephants awoke and saw Apani, and with anger in their hearts, they tore her into little pieces and threw them into the mud. The elephants became even more suspicious of humans after that and left their valley and the old lady in search of a new forest where there were no humans.

This story has many moral dimensions. First, siblings should learn to love each other and avoid unnecessary jealousy. Apani, the elder twin, was nice enough to lend her beautiful necklace to her twin sister, Akuma, but when Akuma lost the necklace, it was unfortunate that her sister was so wicked and unforgiving that she would demand such unreasonable compensation from her sister. Couldn't she have forgiven her for losing a necklace, though it was dear to her heart?

The younger sister showed her love and loyalty to her sister and forgave her for all the troubles she had put her through. When she compensated her for the lost necklace, she had nothing but pure love for her and even allowed her to move into her home with her husband. The elder sister showed that she was not a responsible person, because while in her sister's home she partied with her gold ornaments and precious golden cups without permission from her sister. In addition, she did not care enough to take good care of them and instead broke them. In short she did not display a sense of responsibility toward her sister's property.

Another moral character displayed by the younger sister Akuma was her sense of humility and respect for people. In all her travels she displayed humility to all the strange villagers she met, and they for their part returned to her the respect she gave them and showered her with gifts as well.

Contrary to her younger sister's high morality, the older sister Apani displayed extreme arrogance and lack of respect for the villagers she encountered in her travels. She was so rude in the manner in which she greeted and spoke to the villagers that they were eager to get rid of her. In the long run, her sauciness and abrasive behaviour and her reluctance to follow instructions and work with people led to her own early death.

Answer the following questions:

1. a) How did the two beautiful twins treat each other after their parent's death?
   b) Which of the twins later got married?
2. a) What destroyed the love Apani had for Akuma?
   b) What happened to the necklace Akuma borrowed?
3. a) Why was Apani jealous of her twin sister?
   b) List all the items Apani asked as compensation for her lost necklace?
4. Describe how Akuma was able to get all the items her sister requested as compensation including the tail of the queen elephant?
5. Why didn't Apani compensate Akuma with the same items she had already received from her?
6. How did Apani treat the villagers she met on her expedition?
7. How did Apani die at the hands of the elephants?
8. What have you learned from this folktale?

9. Find the meaning of the following words in the dictionary and use them in sentences of your own.

i. Loaned
ii. Bedecked
iii. Regal
iv. Concealed
v. Muttered
vi. Chaperoned
vii. Euphoric
viii. Intoxicated
ix. Encrusted
x. Summoned
xi. Heirloom
xii. Echelon
xiii. Painstakingly
xiv. Melancholy
xv. Sympathetic
xvi. Exhaustion
xvii. Dirge
xviii. Nuggets
xix. Relentlessly
xx. Tier
xxi. Astonished
xxii. Bellowed
xxiii. Hesitation
xxiv. Slashed
xxv. Shrill
xxvi. Mysteriously
xxvii. Sauciness
xxviii. Astounded
xxix. Yanked